# The Illusion

ò

A Bulwark Anthology
Volume 2

DJ COOPER

This is a work of fiction. Names, characters, places, and events are either the product of the author's imagination or used in a fictitious manner. Any resemblance to actual persons, living or dead, locals or actual events is purely coincidental.
This work is an anthology of Bulwark.

Illustrations by RL Jackson

ISBN-13: 978-1-947188-98-3
ISBN-10: 1-947188-98-4

# DEDICATION

For Phyllis,

the pizza is ready!

# CONTENTS


| | | |
|---|---|---|
| 1 | CHANGING APPEARANCES | 1 |
| 2 | A BRICK TO THE HEAD | 9 |
| 3 | THE WORST PATIENT | 15 |
| 4 | IT'S WET AND IT STINKS | 21 |
| 5 | PERPETUALLY HUNGRY | 27 |
| 6 | DINNER AND A SHOW | 33 |
| 7 | WHEN IS IT? | 43 |
| 8 | JASPER | 53 |
| 9 | AH, PIZZA! | 59 |
| 10 | BEHIND HIS BACK | 61 |
| 11 | BREAKFAST | 63 |
| 12 | WHAT JUST HAPPENED? | 71 |

# 1

## Changing Appearances

"There's something I'd like to show you if you have a minute, Terence." Dr. Peter Kent shuffled his feet uncharacteristically as he addressed the junior police officer behind the station's desk. A phone rang at one end of the room and was answered on the third ring. Another conversation penetrated the awkward pause between the two men. Kent hesitated before continuing in a hushed tone, "I, I er, it's not a police matter. Maybe after your shift?" The young deputy's face reddened slightly. This dance of theirs had been progressing at a slow, torturous pace for months.

Terence nodded. "I finish at four today. Where shall I meet you?"

Dr. Kent felt a slight tightening in his chest and reached for the pen and notepad on the desk with hands shaking more than he'd like. "Text me when you're done. I know you might get caught up. I'll pick you up and drive us out there. It's not far."

Terence raised a single eyebrow in a questioning look. He already knew the phone number Kent had written on the paper. The deputy was intrigued.

Bulwark had its moments, but things had quietened down in the last few weeks. Terence was up for a mystery that involved more than a stray dog and a garbage can. He nodded his consent and looked forward to his early finish on what could be a frantic Saturday.

Kent double tapped the desk with his knuckles. "Great, it's a date. I mean, I'll see you later and show it to you, my thing, I wanna… I mean... later." With wide eyes caused by the nonsense his mouth had just spewed forth, Dr. Peter Kent caught the glare of Sheriff Clay Finnes as he turned to leave. He wondered if the sheriff would ever get it through his thick skull how little threat the doctor posed to his interests, romantic or otherwise. Kent glanced back at the desk and saw the deputy shuffling papers. As the doctor turned to leave, Terence looked up and failed to make eye contact. That just about summed up what they may never get to call their relationship.

"What was that about?" Sheriff Finnes asked as he approached the desk.

The younger man's face flushed a second time as he contemplated his answer, "Oh he wants to show me something after work."

The sheriff grunted in response, "You be careful with him. He has a…" he paused and looked away into the distance, trying to find the word. "He has a reputation."

"Yeah, a false one," the deputy countered. He stopped short of reminding Finnes that he'd been sure the doctor was chasing Finnes' own wife not so long ago. It was a badly kept secret Terence was not supposed to know. It had taken the insistence of Jenna, Finnes' wife that she was definitely not the doctor's type. Yet still, the animosity remained.

"Just be careful with lover-boy," the sheriff said.

"He's not, I mean we're not, never mind." There didn't appear to be much Terence could do to persuade Sheriff Clay Finnes and others of two things, one that Terence wasn't a child and two that Dr. Peter Kent wasn't the devil.

***

Despite the mild winter, cool late-morning air brought Peter Kent's shoulders to his ears as he pulled at the zip on his jacket. Hunched, he rammed his fists into his jeans pockets and walked on autopilot for ten minutes before noting his surroundings. He looked up and shook his head. Why he had gravitated back to the side road he wanted to take Terence to later that day, he didn't know. He stopped in front of the café and shrugged. He shouldered the door, and it gave way and juddered with the grinding noise of door on frame.

"Must get that looked at." The owner was a graying man in his fifties. With hair tied back in a ponytail, he carried a surplus of his own baked goods around his middle beneath the light brown apron Peter had now come to expect. The doctor tried to switch off and not see pastry-induced medical issues in the older man's future. "What can I get you? The usual?" the man asked reaching for a pot of black coffee and a mug.

Peter stopped and shot a look at the man, "I, er, yes, thank you." He hadn't realized he'd been in

Durnley's café often enough to have acquired a 'usual'. "How long have you been here?" he asked. The proprietor stopped pouring from the coffee pot and stuck his bottom lip out as he contemplated his answer.

"Been open, you mean? About eighteen years, I'd say."

"That long?" Peter tried to hide his surprise. The owner of a café should have a better idea of how long the establishment had been open than a customer who had only discovered the place a few days before. As a relative newcomer to Bulwark as Peter was, he would be surprised if he'd found the place before any of his colleagues. They'd never mentioned Durnley's. A timer sounded from the kitchen at the rear of the building. "Smells good," Peter said as Walter Durnley set a mug of hot coffee on the table in front of him and hustled towards the source of the aroma.

Peter muttered, "thanks" and picked up the mug, bringing it to his lips. Hot enough to drink but not hot enough to burn, he took a sip and replaced the mug on the dark brown table. He took a minute to contemplate the long silver and glass counter of lunch options open to him. It was a little early for lunch, but he was used to grabbing food when the opportunity presented itself rather than waiting for a meal-time he'd end up working through.

Unable to make a decision about food, Peter turned away and looked at the wall nearest to him. A picture on the light-yellow wall caught his eye. The tiny print on the bottom right dated the picture fifty years ago but showed Walter Durnley in the doorway of another restaurant looking identical to the way he looked today. Must have been a family member. The doctor stood to appraise the other pictures on the wall. Some he recognized from around town from years gone by and others he did not. A picture of the hospital drew his gaze. The building had changed little in the years Peter had worked there. Something else caught his attention. The clothes people were wearing would now be called 'retro' but an extension to the building he knew was added in the last five years was also featured. Maybe it was a costume party? Although, he'd not heard of any. Peter leaned towards the picture and squinted. Physically, the young police officer in the foreground bore an uncanny resemblance to Terence. Just as Peter dismissed the thought and turned his head, the young officer in the photo seemed to look away. Peter took a step backwards, scraping a chair across the floor as he went. He bumped into another dark brown table which rocked and threatened to upset the metal basket of condiments. In an overreaction, Peter slammed his hands onto the table to prevent its contents from being scattered onto the floor.

"You okay there?" Walter asked as he returned from the kitchen with a tray of lasagne fresh from the oven. Peter's stomach growled. He set the chair back in its rightful place and returned to his table and his coffee.

"Could I have a…" his words were cut short as a plate of the lasagne he was about to ask for appeared in front of him along with a knife and fork. He looked up at Walter and opened his mouth to say thank you as another observation interrupted him. Walter's ponytail had gone to be replaced with short gray hair and his light brown apron was dark green. The apron Peter could have dismissed as being changed for hygiene reasons. The ponytail, he had no explanation for. "Thank you," he finally muttered. Clearly, he had not had enough sleep.

Steam rose from the pasta as Peter's impatient stomach growled again.

"Better eat that while it's hot. More coffee?" Walter asked.

With a forkful of food halfway to his mouth, Peter was part of the way through saying he hadn't finished the first one when he saw his empty mug and said, "yes please" in flat tones. He was sure he hadn't drunk the first coffee. Confused, he took a bite of the pasta as the clock behind the counter struck once. He gestured with his empty fork at the clock to point out the inaccuracy of the timepiece when a hunch stopped him. Finishing his mouthful, he glanced at his own watch. It too said one o'clock. He'd left the police station at around eleven and walked for a few minutes to this quiet road that seemed familiar, yet new to him at the same time. With his back to the kitchen, facing the café's front window he stared through the glass and wondered where the lunchtime crowd was. If he had been there for over an hour, he'd not seen another soul in that time.

Peter looked down at his plate in search of another forkful of lasagne. The plate was empty.

"I see you enjoyed that," Walter said as he took the empty plate and mug and replaced them with a second cup of coffee.

"Thank you," Peter said, looking away. He glanced around the café and felt apprehension and a sudden need to leave. He had definitely not finished his lunch. The light-yellow walls were now blue. The dark brown wooden tables and chairs were silver metal. He saw his open-mouthed, fuzzy reflection in the glass table top before him. The photos on the walls had been replaced with canvas prints of flowers in vases. A motivational phrase hung in a black frame on the wall in place of the clock. Walter Durnley had slicked back, jet black hair and a white apron covering a slim physique. As Peter Kent picked up his coffee cup, the noise reached him from the other tables. Dizzy, he blinked at a haze which seemed to cover his eyes. A young, casually dressed couple held each other's hands whilst using the other to feed themselves the lasagne Peter could not recall eating. A man in a suit sat at another table with a laptop open to one side and a bowl of soup and some bread to the other. In-between gulps of soup he typed and manipulated the work on the screen in front of him. A young mother scolded a child for throwing small packets of sugar onto the floor. Two women sat at another table bent towards the middle where they were deep in conversation. Where had these people come from? He set his mug back on the table and the metal teaspoon he hadn't realized he'd been holding clattered down onto the glass table top. Silence fell over the room as the other patrons noted and disregarded the sound which had interrupted their lunch. The lunchtime café noise resumed.

Gulping the remains of his coffee, Peter retrieved too much cash from his wallet and set it down on the table with shaking hands. Almost upending his chair, he stood in haste and weaved his way through the tables towards the door.

"Your change," Walter called out to Peter's back.

"Keep it. Thanks," Peter replied, standing aside to make way for a middle-aged couple eager to take his newly vacated table. A gust of wind threatened to tear the door from his hand as he stepped outside and pulled it shut. There must have been another door open out the back. Without thinking he stepped into the road causing a car to swerve around him and a horn to sound as the vehicle disappeared around the corner at speed. Peter stepped back and leaned up against the wall with his eyes shut for a few seconds. When he opened them, the sky was gray, and he could almost convince himself he'd witnessed nothing untoward. He turned back to the café. The lights were off, the interior was shrouded by darkness. The long counter holding the many lunchtime choices was empty. The dark brown wooden tables and chairs he'd originally seen were neatly arranged. In the distance towards the back of the café where the kitchen was located, a middle-aged man with a gray ponytail and light brown apron was just visible in the doorway. He stood immobile except for his slowly nodding head.

Peter took a sharp intake of breath and pulled his jacket collar up around his neck as he turned towards the familiarity of the hospital.

# 2

## A Brick To The Head

The normally bright lights of the hospital flickered as Peter absent-mindedly walked, head bowed through the waiting patients. A yelled warning failed to penetrate his brain fog as a shoulder bag which could have contained a brick made contact with his head. He froze, neither fighting nor fleeing away from the impact. *So much for that theory*, he mused. He watched the bag settle on the floor.

Out of the corner of his eye, he registered a behemoth of a man barreling towards him in time to dodge out of the way.

"Doc! You okay?" Deputy Terence Blake called as he and a hospital security guard wrestled the man under control. Peter watched, useless as Dr. Lisa Alvin administered a shot to calm the man and yelled for Dr. Kent to get a gurney. Frozen, Peter watched as someone else jumped into action and provided assistance. He didn't register the concern on the faces of his colleagues as they wheeled the man through the internal doors and the relative privacy of a side bay.

Terence hung back. "Hey, Pete, you alright? How

hard was that impact?" Terence looked but found no bump or break in the skin on Peter's head. "Let's get you checked out. Do you think it's a full moon? It always seems to bring out the crazies." There was no answer and no protest as he led the doctor through the doors to a bed.

Doctors make the worst patients. The thoughts and doubts of the last couple of hours ran through Peter's mind. The bang on his head was the perfect excuse to be examined for any cause of what Peter wanted to call his hallucination. There had to be a medical reason for what he had witnessed that day. Rooms did not dramatically change their appearance and people couldn't just materialize from nowhere then vanish.

Peter's mind filled with Walter Durnley's image. Sporting the ponytail, Durnley stood in the doorway to the kitchen of his café nodding slowly. The action meant nothing to Peter who closed his eyes tight, willing the vision to go away. When he opened his eyes, he took in his surroundings for what seemed like the first time. Propped up on a hospital bed in a bay in the emergency department, the sound of the busy area crescendoed as his mind cleared and his hearing began to function fully.

"Does it hurt?" Dr. Alvin asked, leaning towards Peter to check his pupil response. "You were screwing your face up. Does it hurt?" she repeated. The smell of her shampoo lingered as she straightened and flicked short blonde hair from her face.

"Huh? Er… no. Maybe a bit." Movement drew his

head to the opening in the curtains. His shoulders dropped forwards at the sight of the gathering of co-workers who displayed a mixture of concern for their colleague, and thinly veiled attraction. A couple of them eyed Deputy Blake with disdain as he moved them aside to reach his friend.

Dr. Alvin sighed as she reached for the curtains and issued instructions to the hangers-on. "What is it you do that makes them follow you around like teenagers?" She whipped the curtains closed, shielding them from prying eyes.

"Nothing. I'm just irresistible." Peter's attempt at humor was met by a cold stare from Lisa Alvin. In contrast, Deputy Blake was grateful his blush was largely hidden by his dark skin.

To change the subject, Terence asked, "Is he okay?"

"Seems to be. But I'm going to order a CT anyway to be sure." The resistance Lisa has been expecting from Peter failed to materialize. "So that's what we'll do." She hesitated to give Peter a chance to argue. When he failed to fight her on the issue, she put the order through on a tablet, hiding her surprise at her colleague's acquiescence.

"How long have the lights been flickering?" Peter asked.

"All day. Maintenance is on it but so far they don't know what's causing it," she said. Peter opened his mouth to speak but was cut off, "Before you ask, no other equipment is affected, it's just the lights."

Turning to Terence, Peter asked, "Anywhere else in town affected like this?"

"Not that I've heard. But if everything else is okay at the hospital, it's likely to be something wrong with the lighting circuit here than a problem outside the building, isn't it?"

Peter shrugged his shoulders, "yeah, probably."

A clattering of metal instruments on the hard floor reached them from outside Peter's bay. "Stay put. Don't let him wander off. I'll see what that was," Dr. Alvin said as she left, flicking the curtains closed behind her.

"What time is it?" Peter asked.

"Five past one." Terence looked at his watch then rubbed his stomach as it growled.

"Can't be," Peter muttered to himself. The words, "In the afternoon?" left his lips before he realized the question might raise more concern over his head injury.

"Yeah, why? Are you sure you're alright, Pete?" Terence reached a hand towards Peter's head, but unfamiliar with the processes for examining a head any more than he already had, he quickly withdrew it.

"I'm fine. I probably don't need a CT scan, but seeing as Dr. Alvin has already ordered one…" he left the sentence unfinished. Aware the only reason he had agreed to one was to rule out an anomaly accounting for his visions in the café earlier, Peter took a deep breath and looked away.

"Do you want me to go?" Terence asked shuffling uncomfortably in his chair.

"No. Sorry. Just got a couple of things on my mind, that's all."

Misinterpreting Dr. Kent's mood for anxiety over

his head scan, with no authority in his voice, Terence said, "I'm sure the scan will be fine. It didn't look like the bag hit you that hard. But you do seem a bit… distracted."

"What was in the bag, anyway?"

"A brick."

"Huh. That's what it felt like." Peter paused before squinting and asking, "Why did he have a brick in a bag?"

"Said it was his baby."

Dr. Kent thought for a second before asking, "Did they call psych?"

"Oh yeah, straight away."

The discussion did nothing to alleviate the tension between the two men. Both were relieved when the curtains parted and an orderly with a wheelchair arrived to transport Dr. Kent for his scan. That was fast but Peter didn't trust his mind enough to question how long he'd been waiting.

"While you're gone, I'm going to grab a sandwich. I'm starving." Terence's stomach growled in agreement. "Want anything for when you get back?"

Dr. Kent smiled, "You're always hungry. No, I'm fine thanks. I've already had lunch." Although, to be honest, Peter Kent could not remember having more than a bite or two of lasagne.

# 3

## The Worst Patient

As soon as the CT scan was complete, Peter was up and across the room looking at his own head on a screen. "Yeah, that's fine," he concluded. Despite protests from all around him, he refused a wheelchair and the inevitable wait to be accompanied back to the emergency department and strode off, uncomfortable in his own skin. The lights had been continuing their staccato dance throughout the time he had been in the hospital. A wave of dizziness kept him to the side of the corridor as people passed him. Their faces seemed to elongate then swell before his eyes. Their features stretched grotesquely across their heads as Peter's vision swam. Voices around him became muffled and blackness crept over his field of vision in an ever-increasing shroud.

His eyes were closed, and he was aware he was moving. No, he was being moved. He felt his head drop down onto his chest. Despite not being able to see, Peter was aware of flashing lights to one side of his head. He guessed correctly that he was back in a wheelchair, heading to a destination he assumed was the emergency department.

"These damned lights," Dr. Alvin's voice pierced the haze of her colleague's mind. To anyone in a position to act, she called, "Get on to maintenance again. We can't work like this." Turning to Peter and the orderly who had saved him from collapsing onto the floor, she asked, "What happened to him?"

"He left after the scan. I found him in the corridor and brought him back here."

Through a spray of sandwich crumbs, Terence managed to make his concern audible.

A deep yell sounded from across the emergency department. To the orderly, Dr. Alvin said, "Go and see if they need any help." To Terence, "Deputy Blake, help me get him onto the bed. You'll have to put the sandwich down," she added as he froze at her command. She opened her eyes wide at him and glanced at the table for him to deposit his lunch and help her.

"Yes, Doc, I'll er, yes."

"Peter, can you stand?" Dr. Alvin asked.

A word that could have been "probably" was all Dr. Alvin needed to proceed. It had been a hell of a day, and the situation with the lights was really started to aggravate her usually calm personality.

"Grab an arm," Dr. Alvin instructed.

Words failed to move from Terence's brain to his mouth and he found himself pressed up against the man he'd had a few drinks with. As he helped Dr. Alvin maneuver Peter onto the bed, Terence felt a tightness in his chest. It was a dizzying mixture of concern and something else which rendered him incapable of coherent thought. As Dr. Alvin busied herself around her colleague and patient, she stole glances at Terence and felt for the guy. Poor lamb had it bad. She stifled a smile. Everyone except, it seemed, Dr. Peter Kent and Deputy Terence Blake knew that the two men had a thing for each other. The hospital grapevine would implode if these guys ever sorted themselves out.

"What's going on?" Peter looked from Dr. Alvin to Terence and back.

"Welcome back. Have you eaten today?" Dr. Alvin asked.

"Actually, I'm not sure that I have." Peter cursed himself for his clumsy choice of words which might keep him in the hospital for longer than necessary.

"You said you had," Terence said, wounded that he hadn't been told the truth. The puppy dog look on his face as Terence handed over half his sandwich made Dr. Alvin turn away before her smile could be seen.

"Take it," she said, busying herself with the contents of a drawer she did not require, "You need to eat."

With a mouth of chicken salad on wholegrain, Peter spluttered his appreciation. The lasagne from earlier might as well have been a figment of his imagination. It was a thought which slowed his chewing.

"I'll be back to check on you in a bit," she said glancing from Peter to Terence and away quickly before the proud look on the latter's face threatened her composure again. She took a step beyond the bay and inhaled deeply, schooling her features and preparing for the next patient.

"I can get you another sandwich, if you want," Terence was eager to be of use.

"No, it's… actually, yes please.  And a coffee."

In a rare moment of fortuitous timing, the pair made eye contact and held each other's gaze. That effect that Dr. Peter Kent was rumored to have over the entire hospital swamped Terence into replying with a slurred, "I'll be right back." As he rushed past Dr. Alvin, he managed to mutter the words "more food" by way of an explanation.

"Feeling any better?" she asked reaching Peter's bedside.

"Seem to be. I should go now." A restraining hand on his chest signaled at least one person wasn't under his spell.

"You'll keep your ass firmly on that bed until I say you can go." Where Dr. Kent exuded an all-encompassing attractiveness, Dr. Alvin's striking face knew how to emit a ferocity even Kent wouldn't challenge. Amused, he sat back, still uncomfortable being on the wrong side of the stethoscope.

"My scan looked fine."

"I know." Before Dr. Alvin could continue the jangling noise from a jostled cart of medical equipment announced the return of Terence. He handed over coffee and a sandwich.

"They didn't have chicken. Got cheese." He eyed the packet as Peter ripped it open and removed a handful of bread and cheese. He caught sight of Terence and handed the rest of the packet to him.

"There, eat, I had half your last one." He turned to Dr. Alvin while chewing and said, "Happy? I've had food. I'm not concussed. My scan was clear. I bet there was nothing from the blood work you took either."

"It's not all back yet. Finish your sandwich and you can go. But come back if you start feeling any different." A clang from outside the bay brought a frown to her face as Dr. Alvin turned, "What is it about today? The whole town is throwing its weight around." Before she left, she turned back to Terence, "If you're able, keep an eye on him. If he gets worse, bring him back in."

"Will do, Doc."

Dr. Alvin rolled her eyes at the crumbs Terence was leaving on himself and the bay and left to attend to who knew what outside.

"You alright?" Terence stopped brushing crumbs from his uniform and stared at Peter whose eyes were closed tight as he winced in pain.

"Just a headache."

"Not surprising given the brick to the head. Didn't they give you one of those ice packs?"

"They offered, I declined." It was an action Peter now regretted.

"Can I get you one?" Concern spread across Terence's young face.

"No, let me finish this coffee and we'll get out of here. Thank you for staying with me, but you ought to get back to work before Sheriff Finnes finds out I've been monopolizing your time."

"He's not that bad, he'll understand."

It was a nice sentiment, but not one Peter could fully get behind. He grunted when the lights dimmed and rose again with the accompanying hum. "That is really starting to annoy me."

"Is that because of your head injury?" Again, Terence looked concerned.

"No, it's because it's really starting to annoy me." Peter carefully swung his legs off the bed and pushed himself to a standing position. His head throbbed from the impact but there was no other cause for alarm. He took one step followed by another until he was sure he could walk. Rather impressed with himself he announced to anyone within hearing, "Fairly indestructible." Turning to Terence who had crept up behind him ready to offer assistance if necessary, "Let me know when you've finished your shift and I'll meet you. There's a place I've found that I want you to see."

"Sounds good. Take it easy. I wouldn't go home if you're going to be alone, you should probably have someone keep an eye on you."

"Don't worry, there's a neighbor I can look in on," Peter lied.

# 4

## IT'S WET AND IT STINKS

Out of sight of those who might advise against his actions, Dr. Kent went to his locker and retrieved the sneakers he kept in a bag. His current state made running out of the question but he had to clear his head and despite fatigue, a long walk was what this doctor ordered. He couldn't be around anyone. Company made him uncomfortable, and it was a feeling he wanted to shake before he met Terence later on. He checked his watch. It was well after two in the afternoon. It made no sense given hospital waiting times. It should be much later if he had lunch at one o'clock. His walk wouldn't be as long as he'd hoped but it would have to do. He skirted a group of hospital staff hanging around outside the locker room. It was the same group as earlier. He just couldn't get into it but felt like telling them to get back to work. As he left them behind, he heard a giggle followed by Dr. Alvin's stern voice instructing them to do what Dr. Kent was unable to. He rounded the corner and he caught her distant voice asking, "What has gotten into everyone today?"

Peter walked through the emergency department. The familiarity of the efficiency and professionalism washed over him, soothing him as much as the green walls did when he arrived at work each day. He left, stepping into a misty afternoon. Bulwark was experiencing a mixture of seasons all of a sudden. He pulled his jacket closed around him and thrust his hands into his pockets. Finding his Bluetooth earphones, he threw the connecting wire behind his head and twisted the buds into his ears. A couple of seconds after switching them on, they announced they had connected. He pulled his phone from his pocket and called up a playlist. Cranking up the volume, he needed to be consumed by sound. Other doctors listened to lectures, Dr. Peter Kent listened to a variety of music ranging from the Medieval era to electronic dance music. Today, he needed anything with a beat. Anything to distract him from whatever he was currently experiencing.

Forgetting his intention, he took off at a jog and was halfway through the parking lot before his body reminded him how tired he was. He leaned on a metal hospital sign for balance. He half smiled at two of the medical staff as they walked past deep in conversation, his presence all but unnoticed. By the time they turned to acknowledge his existence, he had resumed at a more sedate pace.

A car honked its horn as his lack of concentration took him into its path. Dr. Kent stared at the front of the blue vehicle inches from his knees and gave the windshield a vacant but what he hoped was apologetic look as he raised his hands and stepped back. He couldn't shake the fog in his brain. There was something about him in this town he had recently moved to that didn't gel. It was as if his scientific mind felt the need to fight something that was inherently Bulwark. He made a noise of disgust to himself as he realized how he sounded and set off down the road. The pounding music in his ears failed to have any detrimental effect on his headache.

***

What should have been five minutes later, Dr. Kent stopped to look around him. His brow furrowed at the deserted unfamiliar road. He pulled the earbuds out and retrieved his phone. He stopped it in the middle of the seventeenth song on his playlist. It was running straight through the list with shuffle deactivated. He'd only been walking for five minutes, ten at the most. Seventeen songs. He had no recollection of how he got there and the only indication of how long it had taken was the number tracks he had apparently listened to on his phone.

As he stared at the screen, the phone began to ring. He caught the call just before it went to voicemail. Despite seeing the familiar name displayed on the screen, he answered officially, "Dr. Kent."

"Er, Doc? It's Terence."

The power of speech failed the doctor, and he stood silently with the phone to his ear.

"Pete?" Interference from somewhere produced a crackle on the line. The use of the shortened version of his name penetrated Peter's consciousness.

"Hi, Terence. Where the hell am I?" Sudden

alertness brought his limbs back to life as he twisted to see where he had come from. He moved his feet. They were wet. Looking down, he saw he was standing on the edge of a pool of green water. He pulled a face as his brain registered its fetid aroma. Looking down at his half-submerged sneakers, he took a few steps back and felt as if his voice had been set free after a long vow of silence.

"Do you know of a treelined road that's flooded? It's not totally underwater. About a third of the way across. Has there been some kind of spill? The water's green."

"What are you doing all the way out on Jericho? I thought you were going to stop in on a neighbor." There was a mixture of hurt and worry in Terence's voice. Worry because Peter hadn't been himself earlier, and hurt because he'd felt it necessary to hide his true intentions from a man who was supposed to be more than just his friend.

"Yeah, I know. I needed to walk and clear my head. Have they sampled this water?" Peter asked squelching a few steps onto drier road.

"Yes, it's got a high concentration of algae. They've drained it a few times. They've dug channels and tried to encourage the water to flow into the trees at the side of the road. Whatever they do, it keeps coming back. One of the oddities of Bulwark." There was a pause in the conversation before Terence continued, "Look, I've just finished. Can you see the main road?"

"Yes."

"Walk back there and turn right. Keep walking and

I'll come and get you. I just need to change clothes."

Peter mumbled "thanks" and the call ended. He walked back along the road listening to the leaves rustle and an unfamiliar bird song. As the stench of the water receded, Peter's mouth remained turned down at the corners as he squelched along in soaking shoes and socks. The occasional whiff of rotting eggs from his waterlogged footwear completed his experience.

A ramshackle cabin he didn't remember passing sat a short distance from the road. Movement caught his attention. He seemed to recall an old local football hero lived there. He'd probably seen him in the hospital or around town. Peter's mind was fuzzy. JB something? He wasn't sure. He raised a hand in greeting to the man who had emerged from the building. JB Something waved back just as a loud bird flew close by and drew Peter's gaze. When he turned back to the old man, neither he nor the cabin was visible. Peter wiped a hand over his eyes and sighed. He was further along the road than he thought. The cabin and its inhabitant were a good thirty yards away from him. He squinted but could no longer see the man outside the cabin. He turned away and continued to trudge along the road to where he would hopefully be picked up by Deputy Terence Blake.

# 5

## PERPETUALLY HUNGRY

By the time Terence pulled up alongside the doctor, the shoes had been removed and Peter was carrying them in one hand angled away from his body. “Pop the trunk, I don’t want to be in the same part of the car as these.”

With his contaminated shoes and socks safely sealed in a plastic evidence bag in the trunk of the deputy’s car, Peter sat in the front seat and fiddled with the heating until warm air blew onto his damp feet.

“What were you doing out there?” Terence asked.

Peter looked out of the passenger window and uttered a distracted “Don’t know.” The self-assured doctor did not want anyone to know he hadn’t a clue how he got there.

“I’ll take you back to your place. You can find some dry shoes and a bucket to put the other ones in.” Terence glanced at the doctor and contemplated returning to the hospital for a further check-up. But they had their hands full following a spate of fights which had broken out across town. The only thing linking the fights were their unprovoked nature and that they happened on the same day. Ordinarily, Terence would still be working if Sherri hadn't taken pity on her fellow deputy and agreed to cover while Terence retrieved the doctor from the outskirts of town.

They drove in silence, punctuated by events unfolding on the police radio.

"It seems everyone who was going to have a fight has had one," Terence said as the list of skirmishes diminished.

"Do you need to get back?" Peter asked, alert once more.

"No, it's fine. They've got it handled."

"Maybe I should check in at the hospital. They might need me."

"If you don't mind me saying, you need new shoes and possibly a clean change of clothes. The smell of that pool lingers." Terence glanced at Peter to gauge his reaction. He hadn't just wanted to blurt out, *By the way, you stink.*

"Watch out!" Peter's hands steadied himself on the front of the car as Terence caught up and slammed on the brakes. They watched as a four-legged animal sauntered across the road with no comprehension its life had ever been in danger.

"What was that?" Peter asked.

"Some kind of deer. I haven't seen one of those in a while."

"It only had one antler," Peter said.

"I know," Terence said as if it was normal.

"The antler was in the middle of its head." Peter

stared across at Terence waiting for him to catch on. When he didn't, Peter slumped back in his seat and uttered a weary, "Take me home, please." There was no way he was going to let on he'd seen anything resembling a unicorn.

***

"Sorry about the mess," Peter said as Terence followed him into his living room. The "mess" amounted to one used empty coffee mug on the coffee table and a small stack of magazines with the top one slightly askew from the others. Otherwise, Peter Kent's house was immaculate.

Terence jumped and uttered a jumble of words to show his surprise as he stepped out of the way of a round automatic vacuum cleaner whirring as it performed its daily duties.

"Some people have a dog who greets them when they get home. You have a… whatever this is." Terence stood still as if his life depended on it.

"You can move. Just don't trip over it." Peter watched as Terence skirted the machine fully expecting an uprising. "It's new. It came with stickers. I haven't decided if I want to have the happy face or the monster face." He looked Terence's wide-eyed stare and knew the monster face would end up on the front of his new machine.

"Ugh, dear god," Peter called from the back of the house. Terence joined him to witness the opening of the evidence bag and experience the full force of the stench from the green water soaked into Peter's sneakers. Outside the kitchen door, Peter tipped the shoes and socks into a bucket and emptied a bottle of disinfectant onto the shoes before filling the bucket with water from the almost boiling kettle. He deposited the bag in the trash can. "I might just leave them there and see if they sprout a new life-form. Are you sure it's algae? It doesn't normally smell like that."

"That's what they said on the report," Terence said. He was greeted by an expletive as Peter stepped barefoot on a sharp stone.

"That stench seems to have permeated everything I'm wearing." He pointed to a cupboard and a coffee machine. "Can you make us some coffee while I take a quick shower?"

"Uh huh," Terence stared at the machine and was relieved to see it was nothing more complicated than a drip filter set-up.

***

Minutes later, with the smell of freshly brewed coffee replacing the fetid odor of the puddle, Peter emerged in clean clothes and dry shoes. He felt almost normal again.

Over coffee and cookies for the perpetually hungry deputy, Peter played down his experience of Walter Durnley's café. "I've not come across it before. But it's quite a nice place to eat, if you're interested."

Terence nodded. He started to brush the crumbs from his shirt but stopped when he remembered how clean and tidy the doctor's house was.

Peter smiled, "It's fine, just brush them onto the floor. It'll give Jasper something to do later."

"You're calling the robot thing *Jasper?*"

"Good a name as any."

"When can we go? I'm hungry."

"You've just had cookies." Peter looked at Terence with wide eyes that softened with laughter lines at the corners when he smiled. It was the most relaxed he'd felt all day. A quiet meal he didn't have to prepare and clear up himself was probably just what he needed.

# 6

## Dinner And A Show

Although Durnley's was licensed for alcohol, Dr. Kent had no intention of adding liquor to the list of potential reasons why he didn't trust his mind. Still, he accepted Terence's offer of being the designated driver for the evening. "You've lived here all your life," Peter began, "Has this street always been," he stopped himself from saying "here" in preference to "like this". They walked from the small parking lot to the front of the line of two-story shops and business premises before Terence stopped and frowned.

"Er. Must have been. I mean, I don't remember Durnley's," Terence hesitated. He seemed to feel the same disquiet Peter had when he'd first discovered the place. It had that look of something that belonged but had never quite been acknowledged or accepted totally. Peter shook the notion from his mind. He was not making sense again. All his training had taught him to be accurate and concise. This wishy-washy nonsense wasn't him. He opened the door -and was surprised to see Walter Durnley still serving front of house. Peter had expected another team of people to take over the evening sitting. Durnley looked as fresh as he had hours earlier.

"Gentlemen, how nice to see you. If you wouldn't mind going straight through to the stairs. Evening meals are served upstairs."

Peter nodded and turned to Terence, "Didn't know there was an upstairs. I didn't notice that doorway earlier." There were indeed two doorways at the rear of the premises. One labeled *staff only*, the other led to a stairway. A dozen steps up, Peter stopped and turned to Terence behind him, "This is a two-story building, right?"

"Yeah, why?"

"More stairs." The men shared a look of mutual amusement and confusion before climbing further up the stairs lined with cornflower blue walls. An occasional step creaked beneath them as they climbed. Peter tried to ignore what he thought he saw ahead of him. Reality did not distort in such a way. Rooms did not get further away from you the more steps you took towards them.

Durnley appeared in front of them. Peter had to be stopped from toppling both him and Terence down the stairs as he began to fall backwards.

"Whoa, careful," Terence complained.

"Gentlemen, if you wouldn't mind following me," Durnley motioned with his hand for them to follow.

"How did he get up here before us?" Terence whispered.

"I don't know. Staff stairs?" Peter shrugged and followed their host.

"But he's… old." Terence's comment made Peter

stop and slowly turn his head in disapproval to the younger man.

"He's only about a dozen years older than me."

"*er*... He's old*er*." Emphasis on the *er*, Terence backtracked before nudging Peter to keep up with the proprietor.

They followed Walter Durnley along a short corridor with a bright blue door at the end. It was no more than a couple of dozen feet away. Photos depicting past establishments run by Durnley lined the wall. The black and white pictures were reminiscent of the ones Peter had seen earlier in the day. At equal intervals along the wall, it didn't take Peter long before he saw the pattern. He pointed to the pictures and turned to Terence, "Tell me what you see."

"It's the same four pictures repeating along the wall and this corridor seems to be going on forever."

Relieved, Peter said, "So it's not just me then."

All Terence could think to say was, "What is this place?"

The ambience of an intimate evening restaurant changed to brighter lighting in the doorway. Glancing behind them, they saw nothing out of the ordinary. They had walked along a short corridor lined with just four black and white photographs. Before either could ask any questions, Durnley pushed open the bright blue door and held it there with his arm. The cacophony he released from within made both men lean backwards in surprise. Expecting such a reaction, Durnley allowed Terence and Peter a few seconds to take in their surroundings. Agog, they leaned forward and stared at the arena before them.

In the middle, on the sandy oval, men wore English Medieval costumes. Some were on horseback while others were being dressed in suits of armor.

"Come, gentlemen, please," Durnley encouraged them further into the area and showed them to a wooden table for two. They lowered themselves onto the thick tree trunks fashioned into stools. Around them sat groups of people, couples, families, groups of friends. All of whom were dressed in period costume to match events taking place in the arena below.

"Ever get the feeling you missed the words *costume party* on the invitation?" Terence raised his voice to be heard and grinned with excitement.

"It doesn't bother you there's no way this…" Peter gesticulated to everything around them, "the whole thing couldn't possibly fit inside the building we entered?"

A brief glimmer of reality threatened Terence's enthusiasm but was brushed away with the arrival of goblets. Despite both men being dressed in jeans and shirts among dozens of people wearing medieval attire, no-one treated them any differently from anyone else.

"Drink up, Pete, this is great," Terence smiled so hard Peter thought his face might split. In his head, he made a gristly estimation of how many stitches it would take to fix. He shook the notion from his mind and raising his voice above the cheering crowd, he attracted the attention of the nearest wench. He hesitated. She reminded him of a member of the group who had been hanging around him at the hospital earlier. He couldn't be sure, so he let it go.

"Can I get some water, please?" he yelled. After a brief pause and a questioning look for what was apparently a strange request, the suitably buxom woman in a low-cut beige bodice and a long green skirt smiled, nodded and left. She returned a short while later with what looked to Peter's untrained eye to be a genuine clay medieval jug. Its feel, however, was more modern-day resin or plastic. The goblet she provided did appear to be wooden.

"Whoa, look at this," Terence took his eyes off the entertainment in the arena and focused on platters of food being brought out from all sides. Peter watched as Terence wasted no time in selecting a cooked leg of some beast and, with a glint in his eyes, tucked into the feast which had been laid on the table between them.

With a shrug, Peter looked around the pile of food and then glanced at the nearby raucous tables.

"Just pick it up with your hands. Everybody else is," Terence yelled.

"I don't even know what animal this is," Peter replied leaning over the mountain of food to make himself heard.

"Does it matter? It's delicious."

"At least none of it looks human," Peter said.

"What?" Terence yelled with grease smeared lips. Peter waved him off and selected a leg of… something. It was good, but it didn't taste like chicken.

The doctor turned his attention to the arena and

two men clumsily mounting horses as if they'd never done so before. He couldn't tell what their armor was made from, but they seemed to be having difficulty moving. Finally, on their horses, at either end of a horizontal divider, they were each handed a lance. After several moments of learning how to balance the long pole in one arm and hold on to the horse with the other, a signal was given. Whether the men were ready or not, the horses began galloping towards each other with no encouragement needed from either man. The riders fought to stay on their mounts while brandishing the unwieldy lance. Roars from the crowd filled the arena as one man was toppled from his horse and lay immobile on the sand. The victor was led around the arena. Relieved of his lance, he raised one arm in the air in triumph.

Dr. Peter Kent's attention was still firmly on the prone man on the ground. The distance was too great for him to determine the state of the rider. From his vantage point, Peter saw no movement. Like many of the surrounding people, Terence stood and cheered. Caught up in the reverie, the deputy was enthralled as much as all those present, except Peter.

Gasps from the audience reached Peter's ears as the rider-less horse reared onto its hind legs before landing heavily with both front hooves on the man's chest. Peter closed his eyes in response. Surely, if he wasn't dead before, he had to be dead now. The doctor in him forced Peter to his feet. It wasn't the automatic response he had expected, he had to fight to stand. Everything in him screamed for him to act yet moving was difficult. Around him, guests were cheering, seemingly oblivious to the potential suffering and loss of life below. Despite wanting to climb down into the arena and check on the man, Dr. Kent still couldn't move.

"Something doesn't feel right," he yelled to Terence who either didn't or chose not to hear him.

"Isn't it great? Fantastic entertainment," the younger man enthused. His grin was almost maniacal as his hands clapped with a force which would render them sore later.

When Peter looked back at the arena, the stricken man had gone, and another set of horses and riders had appeared. He watched as similar outcomes resulted from joust after joust. Some men stood after being knocked down. They were helped out of the arena. Others were less fortunate. Each time Peter suspected someone had died, the removal of their body was somehow executed without him seeing. He never once saw anyone who was unconscious be carried off. A part of him continued to scream internally for him to act, to investigate, to at least see if this was some kind of elaborate illusion. Still, he was powerless to move. All he could do was cheer along with the rest of the crowd. Not quite as fervently, not quite as enthusiastically, but he cheered, nonetheless. He was there but not completely *with* them.

Although the noise did not abate, Peter could hear Walter Durnley quite clearly when he announced it was time for Peter to pay his bill. He reached for his wallet but Durnley shook his head. Around them, those not already on their feet stood, applauded and cheered. Terence raised his arms in the air, soaking up the atmosphere. Unlike Peter, he seemed to know what was coming,

"Come on, Pete. It's our turn. Isn't this great?"

Peter felt the color drain from his face. The people around him seemed to lean in towards him so their heads and faces appeared huge and distorted. He felt dizzy. The arena had an echo that made him hear everything twice. He was jostled by the crowd.

Unable to resist, he bounced from group to group as he made his way through the audience. Staggering down through the levels, he finally made it onto the sandy surface of the arena itself.

"I can't ride a horse." He knew he'd said the words but the men intent on cladding him in heavy armor paid him no attention. "I can't do this." Peter's protestations were ignored. Everything in his mind told him to fight this. He was powerless to resist. Trying to move his arms and legs away from the armor was useless. He was as immobile as the man he had seen die.

Terence was playing to the crowd in-between the attachment of various pieces of armor. Peter willed his head to move to attract his attention. Whenever they made eye contact, all Peter could see was a thrilled, madness on Terence's face. Peter couldn't break through and he couldn't tell Terence of the danger they were in. Despite being in the same vast room, they were currently inhabiting completely different universes.

The doctor had been fitted with armor and was surprised by the weight of it. If this was realistic, he didn't envy anyone trying to move fast while wearing it. He tried again to attract Terence's attention. The noise was both deafening yet somehow, now normal. He saw Terence's movements were also hampered by the armor he had willingly been fitted with. Peter imagined if Terence had been a boxer right then, he'd be bouncing from foot to foot; that energy was still visible under the protective layers. Why were they affected so differently? He thought about the initial drink. It was possible they had been drugged. Yet Terence hadn't appeared to drink much more than Peter before the food arrived.

Peter's thoughts were interrupted by screams of excitement from Terence as they were manhandled onto the horses they had been presented with. As he looked at Terence at the other end of the arena, he fought to do something, anything to stop the madness. He was presented with a lance. As he had suspected, it was heavy and unbalanced, and he had no desire to point it in Terence's direction. But that was exactly what he did. Peter's mind screamed *fall off*. All he managed was to close his eyes as the horses began to gallop. The crowd was on its feet screaming louder as the men approached each other. The doctor was unable to alter the outcome. He lost control over his voice and his body. The lance continued to point towards Terence as the horses brought the men closer together.

A flash of red before his eyes blinded him. Peter felt the impact of Terence's lance on his protected chest. He couldn't breathe. His brain reacted by shutting out the trauma and freezing him in time.

Desperate to process the unexpected situation, he found his thoughts failed him. From another vantage point, Peter saw his own body arc through the air. The flight lasted longer than one would expect having been knocked off a horse. A random thought filled his mind that he lacked the experience of falling from a horse to know how long it took. Suddenly blinded and disorientated, Peter didn't know which way he was facing. When he landed, he felt his face and his back impact with the ground simultaneously. He had a sense of completing his mission. Around him, something seemed satisfied with his efforts. The roar of the crowd became distant as Peter was aware of once again seeing the world from where his body lay as the darkness dragged him away.

# 7

## WHEN IS IT?

"Seems to be closed," Terence tried the door to Durnley's café a second time in case it was stuck. "I can't see a sign either way. Are you sure it's supposed to be open tonight?"

Peter opened his eyes but said nothing. He glanced around him. They were standing outside the café. He put a hand to his chest. It felt sore. He checked his watch. It was the time he expected to have arrived at the café.

"Hey, what's up with your chest? You're not having a heart attack or something, are you?" Terence frowned at the wide-eyed look on the doctor's face.

The strength disappeared from Peter's knees and they buckled beneath him. He slid down the café window and sank to the ground. Terence was temporarily a frozen witness. Agape, he watched for a few seconds before recovering his senses. He squatted down in front of Peter, alarm etched on his face.

"Do you need an ambulance? What's going on?" Terence reached a tentative hand towards his friend.

He withdrew and thrust his hand into his pocket to retrieve his phone. Within a few seconds, he was on the brink of issuing instructions for an ambulance for a possible heart attack. Coming to his senses, he realized the small town wasn't overly equipped for medical emergencies. A quicker option would be to take Peter to the hospital in Terence's own car. He stood and looked around. The street was deserted. Shops had long since closed for the evening. The darkened windows hid their merchandize from view. Street lights shone up and down the road, but their glow gave Terence a feeling of cold isolation rather than comfort.

He crouched back down. Peter hadn't moved. A nearby street light afforded Terence enough illumination to see Peter frozen and still clutching his chest, his pale face was fixed in fear. "Dammit," Terence muttered. He placed a hesitant hand on Peter's cheek and tried to force the other man to make eye contact. "Don't move, I'm going to get the car." Terence pushed to his feet and ran to the corner. He glanced back, unsure if seeing Peter in the same position was a good thing or not.

After a quick sprint to the car, he fumbled his keys. He punched a fist onto the roof of the car as he successfully unlocked the door and slid behind the wheel. The engine started and a screech of rubber on road broke the silence as Terence drove to the exit of the parking lot and around the corner to where he had left Peter.

As he slammed on the brakes, his body jolted forwards and back, pushing him into his seat.

Momentarily, he sat with his mouth wide open and eyes darting from one side of the road from the other.

Peter had vanished. Terence threw the car door open with a creak of aging metal and climbed out. Running to the café he tried the door. It was still locked. Just in case there was someone inside who might have seen Peter, he pressed his forehead against the glass with his hands forming a visor around his eyes. The building appeared empty.

"The place around the corner is closed too."

With a grunt of surprise, Terence smashed his forehead against the window before turning towards the voice. Peter. Terence's jaw dropped open in shock and his voice failed him.

"What?" Peter asked, unsure what to make of the expression on Terence's face. "You look like you've seen a ghost." He joined Terence at the window and screwed up his face as he stared through the glass. He couldn't see what had put the shocked look onto his friend's face. Frowning, Peter looked at the younger man, "Tell me what's wrong?"

"Right back at ya, Pete!" Terence countered. To answer the look of confusion on Peter's face, Terence blurted, "You were on the sidewalk staring into the distance with a scary look on your face clutching your chest. I thought you were having a heart attack."

Peter paused for a moment, seeking a logical explanation for the words he had just heard. Finding none, he shrugged and shook his head, "Er…" was all Peter could manage given the unexpected turn in the conversation. "No…," he said when he'd found some composure, "I walked around the corner to see if the diner was open, but it's closed for renovations."

The two men stared at each other as if expecting the other one to back down and claim some kind of practical joke. Neither gave in.

"Maybe we ought to get you checked out at the hospital," Peter said. Terence shook his head and insisted he was fine. Shuffled feet and furtive glances lasted a few too many seconds for either to remain comfortable. Peter sighed, "Look, I'm really hungry," he paused. If they really had been at some kind of feast, hunger wasn't something he should be feeling.

"Way ahead of you," Terence muttered, tapping at his phone. "I'm ordering takeout pizza. We'll pick it up and take it to your place." His youthful eagerness was suddenly replaced with doubt. Turning his head away only highlighted his discomfort as he questioned his brazenness.

Peter rubbed at his stomach and winced. He'd have to take a look to be sure, but he felt bruised. Despite being given the all clear at the hospital after he took a bagged brick to the head, doubts had crept in. He seemed to be living simultaneously in several different realities. The memories of the arena were too real to not have happened. Yet… he stifled a sigh and saw Terence's uneasiness. He gave what he hoped was a genuine smile. "Great. Love pizza." He tentatively rubbed his stomach as if to reiterate the fact he was hungry.

Terence's face lit up. In the growing darkness, his elevated mood was made more apparent by the quick movement of his hands and shuffling feet than his smile.

***

The still evening gave way to a light breeze chilling them with its cold edge. A few drops of rain landed on Peter's face freeing him from the remainder of his stupor. He took hold of Terence's elbow and turned him back towards the car. "Pizza." The word was issued as an instruction. Raindrops increased in size as the men climbed into the shelter of the car. The awkward silence was broken by a crescendo of droplets on metal.

Placing his hands on the wheel, Terence glanced towards Peter for his professional reassurance. "Do we need to get checked out at the hospital? I mean, you really did look like you were having some kind of heart attack."

"I really wasn't," Peter said, staring straight at Terence who couldn't hold his gaze.

"So, who's right?" Terence started the engine and put the car in drive. "We can't both be right," he mumbled.

Peter remained silent and focused on the water running down his window. He looked closer. "Before we go, does that rain look green to you?"

Before looking out of his own window, Terence screwed his face up and gave Peter an exasperated look. "I don't need any more unexplained dramas tonight."

"You think you've got problems," Peter muttered under his breath.

"Sorry?"

"Nothing," Peter slapped his hands down on his thighs and rubbed them, trying to relieve the cold. "Pizza," he called out, attempting to lighten the mood and pointed both hands forwards, away from their local pizza joint. Terence swung the car around. A slight screech from the tires brought a "whoa" from Peter as they headed in the right direction for dinner.

"Looks like their drains have been overwhelmed." Terence cut the engine and looked at the water running down the side of the road.

"How? That was hardly enough rain to water a cactus." Peter unclipped his seatbelt and opened his door to inhale an enticing mix of herbs, tomatoes and various toppings. There was an aroma he couldn't place. Outside Jack's Pizza, the takeout's illuminated sign flickered. A group of women left carrying pizza boxes. They saw Dr. Peter Kent climb out of the deputy's car and one by one stopped. Their heels performed a staccato clicking sound on the sidewalk.

Peter's attention was drawn by the familiar cackle and shriek of inebriation he had witnessed so often in certain patients in the hospital. He raised his eyes to acknowledge what he thought were the voices he had heard earlier. A breeze whipped at the long black hair of one of the women.

Cold dread trickled down Peter's spine like icy water and he shuddered. The black-haired woman turned towards him. Her face morphed into that of an angry hag. Her hair instantly gray and straggly, hung in filthy matted lengths clinging to her face of open weeping sores. Her stench penetrated his nostrils so deeply he could taste her.

The hag's face distorted into a scream and zoomed towards him on an impossibly long neck. He closed his eyes and willed the image away. He would forever regret the sharp intake of breath which filled him with her fetid smell. He dropped his face towards his chest. Unable to see the spectacle, his nostrils were still polluted by her decay.

"What's wrong?" Terence strode around the car and was by Peter's side before the other man had found the courage to face whatever was before him. "Are you in pain? What is it?" Terence clamped his hands around Peter's upper arms and watched as the shaking man slowly raised his head.

"Nothing's wrong." Peter's voice was too shrill to be believable. "I think I just need something to eat and drink," he deflected. A glance over towards the women showed nothing out of the ordinary. No hags, no matted hair, no rotting flesh. Just a woman with long flowing black hair out with her friends. Peter inhaled as he looked at her. She smiled. His brain and nostrils registered the scent of decomposing flesh. He was unable to stifle a shudder or explain the presence of the smells. "Mmmm, smell that pizza," he said. He hoped Terence would counter with something like, "Actually something smells terrible out here." Instead, Peter was met with,

"Yeah, I know, I hope ours is ready." Terence gave the doctor a sideways glance, not trusting the man's assurances. They approached the group of women who giggled and spoke behind their hands to each other.

"They're like kids," Terence complained. "Do you

know them?"

"Don't think so. Although I thought I saw them earlier at the hospital." A sound caught Peter's attention. He turned towards the women to be met with a high-pitched incoherent jabbering and *that* hideous face. He closed his eyes again and swallowed the bile rising in his throat. "Do you smell that?" he turned to Terence.

"Yeah, you can't beat the smell of pizza. Pete? What's wrong?" Terence stopped and reached out to Peter as the man paled and swayed with closed eyes. "You look really green in this light. Come on." He guided his staggering friend into the aroma-filled restaurant and was met with little resistance as he pushed Peter into a chair.

When Peter opened his eyes, his vision was filled with a can of soda and a bread stick. He tried to shake his head. His hearing was fuzzy like he was caught in the drone of high winds whooshing past his ears. The bread stick and soda did not disappear from his line of sight. He relented. A persistent Terence wasn't going to let him move without eating and drinking something.

Peter's compromised hearing continued as he swallowed some cola. He waited for the unmistakable need to run to the door, so he could throw up outside. Nothing happened. Taking another bite, voices from the counter reached him. As his hearing returned to normal, Peter looked up to see a worried Terence and an eagle-eyed Jack. Her hair was tied back in a ponytail while she kneaded dough as her fiancee Alison alternated between glancing at Peter and concentrating on the human fingers and toes she was chopping. Peter closed his eyes tight again. He was hallucinating. He was sure. He took a breath and opened his eyes to look through the glass of the counter. The image of chopped fingers and toes was gone and was replaced by one of Alison chopping a human nose into small pieces. He continued eating and took another gulp of cola. He felt a resolve slipping away from him. Glancing at the counter again, the nose had gone. Alison had a different appendage on the chopping board. As her knife sliced through the human flesh, part of Peter's mind shut down in defense.

"Feeling better?" Jack asked, stepping in for Terence and amused by his stunned silence as the deputy exhausted his repertoire of sympathetic phrases.

Playing along and not wanting to draw attention to his slippery grip on reality, Peter saw the eyeball Alison had picked up from a container and issued an automatic, "Yes, much better thanks." His current state would only improve after food, drink and a good night's sleep. And he was sure the food did not contain human body parts. It wasn't possible.

Terence picked up their order as Peter sat, forlorn on his chair as helpless as the day he was born. Although he hated the situation, Peter had no energy to do anything about it. He rose from his seat too quickly and questioned if he'd learned anything from his extensive medical training. Hearing and dismissing the various "careful" and "steady" calls from Jack, Alison and Terence, he staggered to the door to open it for Terence who was laden with more food than Peter felt he could eat in a week.

Wooden legs carried Peter to the car after mumbled words thanked Jack and Alison for the food and concern. His late thirties body was doing a damned good impression of someone double his age. Peter groaned as he lowered himself into the passenger seat.

Without a word, Terence started the engine and drove them back to Peter's house.

# 8

## JASPER

"I don't remember leaving that light on." Peter reached for the switch inside his front door and in a reflex action, plunged them into darkness before realizing what he'd done and reversing his actions.

"What was that?" Terence juggled the food while leaning against the front door to shut out the night.

"Probably just Jasper." Peter caught sight of his pale face in the hall mirror. Pronounced dark circles had appeared beneath his eyes which seemed to have retreated further into his skull. His cheekbones were more visible as if he hadn't eaten in days.

"Huh?" Terence returned empty-handed from somewhere beyond the hallway. "Oh, the robot floor thing. No, it's not that. *It* is sitting at the side of the room looking threatening." Terence paused as a thought occurred to him. "When did you get around to sticking the monster face on it?"

Peter's shoulders dropped. He cursed himself for not having as good a grasp on the day as he expected. He didn't do ineffective, forgetful or incompetent. "I didn't."

They walked into the living room and stared at the glow-in-the-dark cartoon monster face adorning the cleaner.

"Those aren't the stickers it came with."

"Must be."

"No." Peter bristled. "Look," he reached into a drawer and brought out a plastic bag containing the gadget's instructions. "See," he pulled out two sheets of stickers. "Both sets are still there."

Terence looked at the stickers and back at Peter's face. He hesitated, unsure what to say.

"What?" Peter asked looking at the stickers and thrusting them towards Terence.

"Why don't we sit down and eat before all the cheese congeals on the pizza," Terence evaded.

Aggravated, Peter dropped the stickers on top of the cabinet and walked to the couch. He slumped into the seat and looked around for the food.

"I put it in the kitchen, hang on." Terence glanced at the sheets of stickers on the way to the kitchen. Something wasn't right. He was out of his depth and needed backup. Plucking his phone from his pocket, he unlocked it and punched at a stored contact. When the call was answered, in hushed tones, he explained the situation, obtained the reassurance he sought and replaced the phone in his pocket. He turned towards the living room and jumped.

"Shit, Pete, I thought you were sitting down." Seeing the menacing look on Peter's face, Terence fought to keep his hand away from the weapon he was almost never without.

Peter's lips curled in a snarl, "I'm hungry," he took

a step towards Terence, not breaking eye contact. He snatched a pizza box from the table with a growl and pulled his head back as if he was about to spit in Terence's face. Changing his mind, Peter turned and walked back into the living room. The predatory animal had secured its prey. Terence shook the notion he was about to be spat at from his mind and retrieved the rest of the food. Like a condemned man, he trudged into the living room to resume the evening he had hoped might take their relationship beyond that of mere friendship.

Feeling more comfortable in an armchair than next to Peter on the couch, Terence placed the boxes on the coffee table. He touched a pile of magazines to make more room and received a growl for his trouble. "I'll just move them here." He moved his hands slowly, straightening the magazines in line with the edge of the table. Terence felt his heart rate rise as he continued reasoning with Peter like he was a wild animal contemplating moving in for the kill. "Okay?" The young man raised his hands slowly, palms forward. Deep breaths shuddered in and out of his body as every fiber screamed for Terence to run. The situation was ridiculous. Peter was no threat. He was a doctor for god's sake. He saved lives for a living. He did not end them. But in that moment, Terence had never felt so vulnerable in his presence.

They sat in silence staring at each other. Terence tried to keep his face as neutral as possible. Anything to not provoke the man before him. Peter's erratic breathing and wide-eyed feral stare held Terence's gaze. An almost imperceptible growl accompanied each of the doctor's exhalations as he slowly turned his head towards the automatic vacuum cleaner. Terence looked at the docking station where Jasper sat. The deputy's mouth dropped as the cleaner jolted forward a few inches and turned in his direction. Terence half-turned his head back in acknowledgement of the loud growl from Peter. The deputy's gaze snapped back to the sleek black cleaner as it sprang to life again and shot forward a few more inches. Another growl from Peter seemed to be an instruction for the device to edge further towards Terence. A notion the deputy found to be ridiculous even in Bulwark formed in his mind. *Don't show it fear. Do not show you are afraid. Don't show weakness.* A logical internal voice uttered *what's it going to do? Clean you to death* and was silenced by growing panic as the whirring built in volume. Peter's growls grew more urgent, something inside the cleaner grated loudly and the disk nudged further into the room. Terence froze as something snapped and the cleaner rolled across the floor towards him.

The young man yelled in shock at the sound of the doorbell. His arms shot upwards in a Moro reflex he should have left behind in infancy. He clambered out of his seat as his surprised yell brought hammering on the front door. Silently, Peter followed.

Not daring to look at Peter or the vacuum cleaner, Terence took the few steps towards freedom and quelled his unease at putting another human at risk from… He had no names for this situation. He opened the door with a sigh of relief.

"Lisa, nice surprise. What brings you out here?"

Peter's relaxed, cheerful face turned to confusion as he saw Terence's unease in front of him and the questioning look on Dr. Lisa Alvin's face. "Come in. The pizza is still warm. There's enough for a small army," Peter said over his shoulder as he walked back into the living room to his place on the couch.

As Terence followed, he tapped the cabinet where Peter had left the two sheets of stickers. One full smiley face set he would have much preferred to see on Jasper the cleaner. And one cartoon monster set in outline only, stickers removed. He glanced across the room to the appliance with the monster face that Peter had taken to calling Jasper. It sat dormant on its docking station. Lisa Alvin nodded in understanding that despite Peter's insistence to the contrary, he or someone else had removed the stickers from the sheet and had placed them on the gadget.

"How are you feeling after that bang to the head earlier, Pete?" she asked setting a medical bag on the floor out of sight.

"Nah, it's fine. I can't even feel it now." He smiled a genuine smile and tapped the seat beside him for her to join him. "Here, eat some. We've got loads."

Lisa sat and glanced over at Terence who was rigid in his chair as if expecting bad news. Peter cleared his throat and Terence's sudden jerk of arms and legs drew the attention of the other two diners. Peter's countenance had returned to normal. He swallowed a mouthful of pizza and smiled at Terence. Nothing in Peter's face gave the other man cause to believe the smile was anything other than affectionate. Yet, Terence was still nervous.

"I could do with a hot drink," Lisa rose to her feet, "anyone else? No, sit down, I'll get it," she rested a hand on Peter's shoulder, as he got up to walk to the kitchen, "Terence can give me a hand."

# 9

## AH, PIZZA!

Left alone in his living room, Peter continued eating. He smiled as he looked down at the pizza. The toppings were exactly what he needed. A roughly chopped human toe, sliced lengthways had been artistically placed on his latest slice. The bone had been carefully removed and the sparse flesh was lightly cooked on the inside surrounded by a deliciously crisp skin on the outside. He was impressed by the sauce. A thick combination of warm blood had been mixed sparingly with the traditional tomato and herbs, which frankly, had probably seen its day when it came to pizza sauces. He hoped this new trend continued. The human ear was a little chewy. He placed it on the lid of the box, much preferring the fleshy thing he had yet to identify. The cylinder of cooked flesh possessed a juicy, yet firm texture and he scouted around the other boxes to see if there was another he could take before the other two came back in.

# 10

## Behind His Back

In the kitchen, Terence's shoulders slumped with relief. He hadn't realized how much tension he had been carrying in his body. "It's like he's a different person now you're here. The whole house feels different." He did not want to reveal his unease with the automatic vacuum cleaner or the absurd notion that Peter could control the device with his mind. The thought made Terence consider he was losing his own.

Lisa busied herself retrieving cups, and given the hour, decaffeinated coffee from various cupboards. Terence gave her a suspicious look.

"Relax." She poured hot water into the mugs. "I stayed here last year while my plumbing was out. Oddest thing, green water everywhere. They fixed it without know why or how it got into the pipes. Apparently, it just sort of appeared then disappeared."

On the other side of the door, unseen by Terence and Lisa, Dr. Peter Kent listened in on their conversation with a look of disdain across his face. He blinked slowly. Hearing they were almost ready to bring the coffee in, he crept back to the couch, sat down and picked up a crisp, browned baby's hand from the pizza and began to eat.

"Great, thanks. I don't think I've drunk enough today." Peter took a mug and smiled.

"How's the pepperoni?" Lisa asked.

"Oh yeah, that's really good," Peter grinned. "They must be using some new ingredients."

# 11

## Breakfast

Peter awoke with a sudden jolt. Eyes wide, he took in his surroundings. He was at home, in his bedroom. A quick glance across the bed filled him with disappointment; he was alone. There wasn't time to take this thought further. A tentative tapping on the door drew his attention. He was groggy with sleep and had a vague idea who it might be. Self-consciously, he pulled the covers up to his neck but reasoned he'd probably had help stripping down to his underwear last night. He couldn't remember undressing or much of anything if he was honest. He frowned and quickly stole a look at the circular bruise radiating from the center of his torso. A bruise that might have resulted from an impact with a round, blunt object such as the lance Terence had been wielding in the 'hallucinations' Peter had experienced upstairs in Durnley's yesterday.

The bedroom door opened enough for Terence to stick his head into the room. Seeing Peter awake and looking towards the door expectantly, Terence ventured in carrying a mug of coffee. "How are you, um, feeling?" He put the mug on the bedside table.

Peter paused before answering, organizing thoughts into some sort of order and realizing he had blanks for some of his most recent memories. "I'm fine, I guess. What happened last night?"

Terence drew in a deep breath and opened his mouth to answer before closing it and trying again. "Well, you told us about your, er, well the… that you think…"

Peter closed his eyes, raised his eyebrows and a hand to stop Terence in his tracks. "Don't worry, it's coming back to me now." He reached for the coffee and mumbled a "thanks". The coffee smelled better than it tasted and failed to live up to its reputation as something to help him wake up. Yet still, he drank it like he always did. "Lisa was here," Peter blurted. "What did she make of all this?"

"Well," Terence blew out a breath recalling the tense words, "If Lisa had her way, you'd be in the hospital right now under observation. Somehow you managed to convince her to let you stay here. I don't know how you did it. Halfway through Lisa telling you she was going to call in the ambulance, and drag you in, she seemed to go quiet. You didn't say much, but she said you gave a convincing argument and as long as I stayed with you, you could stay here. Before she left, she said she thought you needed a good night's sleep. When we looked back at you on the couch, you were already asleep. We managed to wake you up enough so I could half carry you up the stairs and we got you into bed. She left shortly afterwards. I slept on the couch." Terence rubbed his belly. "I've looked in your refrigerator. You do realize you have nothing in for breakfast?"

"Yeah, I usually pick something up on the way into work."

"It's Sunday and neither of us is on duty today, I've checked. Get dressed, I'm taking you out for breakfast."

The thought filled Peter with a mixture of feelings. Food was an excellent idea. He had concerns over the venue.

***

The reassuring sight of pizza boxes in the trash calmed some of Peter's trepidation after he'd showered, dressed and made his way downstairs into the kitchen with his empty coffee mug. A vivid flashback overwhelmed him and he grabbed the countertop to steady himself.

"You carry on like that and I'm taking you straight to the hospital." Terence's eyes were wide with concern.

Peter took a steadying breath and shook his head. "What was on the pizza last night?"

"Pepperoni on one and the full-on meat extravaganza on the other. Why? I don't think there was anything wrong with them. I had some of both and I feel fine."

Peter gave Terence a humorless smile he hoped was more reassuring than he felt. He couldn't get the image of him crunching down on a crispy, cooked baby's hand out of his mind. It was a preposterous notion but he couldn't shake it. "It's nothing. I need breakfast, come on."

"By the way…" Terence paused, something at the back of his mind was gnawing away at him but he couldn't bring it to the fore. Something to do with that floor sweeper thing. Whatever it was, Terence couldn't put it into words. He only managed, "I think that new vacuum cleaner of yours has a malfunction. I can't… I can't remember why I think that." Terence frowned while Peter gave him a warm, knowing smile and placed a hand on his shoulder. He didn't question Terence's observation.

"Don't worry, I know a guy. I'll have it looked at. If it's busted, I'll take it back."

Peter walked through the living room passing Jasper the cleaner on the way. The device clicked and whirred and despite not remembering why he felt that way, Terence's unease around the appliance made him jump and follow Peter quickly to the hallway.

Back in his car, Terence tried to hide his elevated mood since leaving Peter's house. Some unfathomable atmosphere pervaded the building of which only he seemed aware. He glanced at Peter in the passenger seat and pushed away a sensation of disquiet. However, none of Lisa Alvin's basic neurological assessments or blood pressure tests had thrown up anything untoward.

"Where are we going?" Suspicion crept into Peter's voice as he recognized the side road Terence turned into.

"You said you wanted to take me there, I imagine it opens for breakfast." Terence pulled into a parking space.

Quite a few vehicles had already been left in the small parking lot as Terence climbed out and waited for Peter to do the same.

"You alright, Pete?" Terence frowned as the doctor gave him a smile of reassurance which failed to reach his eyes.

The door of Durnley's café opened to reveal lively chatter from the patrons and delicious aromas from the kitchen.

"Guys, nice to see you again." Durnley's gray hair was pulled back into a loose ponytail at his collar. Somewhere in Peter's subconscious, Walter Durnley's use of the word 'again' sounded alarm bells. Terence didn't seem to notice. Peter took in a deep breath on hearing Durnley's next words,

"If you wouldn't mind making your way upstairs, there are free tables available. I'll be with you shortly," he smiled.

Peter saw a glazed look pass over Terence's features. He couldn't describe it any better. The deputy's smile was wide, his pinpoint pupils were tinier than the current lighting encouraged. Peter wiped his clammy hands down the sides of his jeans. He didn't feel right.

"Great, thanks," Terence started for the back stairs, shooting a look over his shoulder to see Peter trudge towards the stairs after him.

A dozen steps led to the upper level. A dark wooden floor easily provided room for eight wooden tables, only one of which was already occupied. The light-colored walls brightened the room but unnerved Peter who had expected something different.

"Looks great," Peter muttered in what he hoped were positive tones. They sat at a table in view of the stairs and picked up the menus provided. Walter Durnley approached them from the other end of the room, causing Peter to glance in alarm at the stairs he knew Walter hadn't used. Terence was oblivious and sat with a grin on his face.

Perusing the menu, the deputy's face lit up further, "I'll have a Walt Special, please and coffee."

Without checking to see what a Walt Special was, Peter said, "I'll have the same, thanks."

"The special is proving very popular this morning. Just give me a few minutes and I'll have you fellas tucking into the best breakfast Bulwark has to offer."

Peter forced a smile for politeness and Terence's sake. The café looked normal. He hadn't examined them in detail, but if pushed, he'd have to say the other diners looked normal too. Terence had the same air of excitement about him as he had the last time Peter had thought they'd eaten at Durnley's. The deputy was adamant the place was closed last night. Peter was supposed to have hallucinated or dreamed or something. Durnley said, "again" like they had been there together before.

"Pete? Pete are you alright?"

When Peter took his hand away from the bridge of his nose to answer Terence, the deputy wasn't paying him any attention. Peter registered a large cooked breakfast in front of the other man. He looked down to his own plate and scraped his chair away from the table in shock. A bloodied human leg lay on his plate with a ridiculous sprig of herbs carefully arranged on the side. A huge chunk of flesh surrounded by bite marks was missing from the leg. He could taste bacon in his mouth and half his coffee appeared to be drunk. He turned to see what had caught the attention of the deputy.

"Such a shame," Terence muttered.

Their table was one of several positioned in a semi-circle above Bulwark hospital's trauma room. Diners sat at each table alternating between feeding their mouths with severed limbs and their eyes with the unfolding medical drama beneath them. Peter recognized his mother on the table below. He saw himself as a small boy after the accident which had left him alive but robbed him of his mother.

"Mom," the adult observer crumpled into his seat. He barely registered the timing was off. A present-day Sheriff Finnes stood on the periphery overseeing the attempts to save Peter's mother. Someone tried to remove the young boy from the area. The youth kicked and screamed and refused to be led away. Somewhere in the back of Peter's adult mind, he knew how wrong it all was. His mother hadn't died in Bulwark. Sheriff Finnes could only have been a child himself when the accident happened. Peter was aware of a dampness on his cheeks as what he thought were tears cascaded down his face and an intermittent beep of medical machines below him changed to a steady flat-line.

# 12

## WHAT JUST HAPPENED?

"Hey, it's Dr. Kent. Doc? Hey, Doc. Wake up. What are you doing here?" JB Straton picked up the doctor's phone and answered the frantic deputy on the other end of the call. "He's breathing, Terence. Actually, he looks like he's sleeping. Darndest thing. Doesn't look like the same type of unconscious I saw as a ball player. Saw a few of them in my time. I'll stay with him til you get here."

Peter's eyes snapped open. He felt damp. No, he felt wet. He pulled a face of disgust as he tried to get up.

"Yup," JB said, "you chose a great place to drop. Right in the middle of the Jericho puddle. Steady."

Without much assistance from JB, Peter regained his senses and some strength and hauled himself to his feet. Unsteady, he held onto JB's arm for a moment. He checked his watch. It was Saturday, just after four in the afternoon.

Deputy Terence Blake pulled up alongside the two men. Careful to not spray green water over either of them, he pulled the car to a gentle stop and climbed out. Still in his uniform, he radioed in to say he was now off duty. "Pete? What the hell? What happened?" Terence turned to JB, "Thank you. He called me, said hello and then nothing."

A cold and wet Peter shivered. Unable to form words of gratitude to either companion, Peter allowed himself to be led to the car.

"I'm getting you checked out." Terence said guiding Peter towards the vehicle. "If, and only if there's nothing wrong with you, we'll go to Durnley's for dinner tonight. I'll order pizza if you're not up to it."

Peter stopped dead in his tracks, shuddered, and fought the wave of darkness threatening to overwhelm him.

The End

# AUTHOR'S NOTE

A huge thank you must go to Brit Lunden for entrusting me with Dr. Peter Kent and Deputy Terence Blake. Your encouragement, advice, and kind words have always meant so much to me.

Writing within another author's universe was not a decision I took lightly. I had fears it would all go horribly wrong or worse, I'd fail to find the words. I hope I've breathed life into the characters and created an enjoyable, additional dimension to the town of Bulwark. (Even if the pizza toppings were a bit dubious!)

Many thanks to RL Jackson for the excellent cover graphics. If the task had been left up to me, you'd have got a black cover with white writing on-I'm *that* good at art.

To my kids, Gemma and Matt, thank you for your quiet encouragement in reading some of my stories, and for claiming to have enjoyed them! To my friend Gray, thank you for continually telling me to keep writing over the years. Finally, to my husband Danny, thank you for your patience, and for always letting me get on and do my own thing. Especially when my own thing isn't necessarily the responsible or sensible thing to do.

***

## Also by DJ Cooper

## Missing Remnants

For more on my books or to get in touch with me–

Visit my website-
https://djsworld.co.uk

Like my Facebook page-
facebook.com/DJCooperFiction

Follow me on Twitter-
twitter.com/BarkingMadDJ

Follow me on Instagram-
instagram.com/barkingmaddj

Read my work on Medium:
medium.com/@debzcooper

Catch up with me on GoodReads:
goodreads.com/author/show/17385792.D_J_Cooper

Discover more of my writing on Amazon:
amazon.com/DJ-Cooper/e/B07CS58S9C

Huge thanks to cover designer
R.L. Jackson
authorrljackson.com

Read on for the first chapter from
The Craving, Volume Four of
The Bulwark Anthology

# The Craving

RL Jackson

# 1

## CHAPTER ONE

The university campus was hoping with excitement as students headed towards different parties to celebrate the start of spring break week. Savannah Daniels sloshed across the damp grass blades on the quad. It was cooler than normal for a Florida night and the short cut off jeans, yellow tank top and flip flops she wore was no protection against the chill she felt on her skin. She rushed towards Beta Lambda Delta, her boyfriend Marshall's frat house to join in the festivities of the pre-spring break party he'd been obsessing about for weeks. Everyone on campus would be there no doubt. It was the party frat house and anyone who was anyone wanted an invite. Savannah didn't normally go to those parties or any others, intent on keeping her head in the books, but she needed to let her hair down and just have fun tonight.

A skateboarder barreled by her on the sidewalk, music blaring through his headphones and side swiped her, knocking her ass to the ground. She hit the damp grass with a thud, the duffel bag she carried on her shoulder with a weeks worth of clothes on top of her. She looked in the skateboarders direction and he had continued about his business. He didn't even look back!

"Asshole!" Savannah screamed, still sprawled on the lawn. She sat up and started getting up when a hand reached down in front of her and the hairs on her arms stood up. She looked up at the man staring down at her and he wasn't someone she knew or recognized. He was too young to be a teacher, but looked more mature than a student. She grabbed his hand, embarrassment washing over face.

"Are you OK?" he asked. His voice was deep and baritone, his eyes so gray they were almost white. Her head felt a little tingly, almost dizzying as she stared into the pools of his eyes.

"I'm fine," Savannah replied, taking her hand back.

"You have to be careful out here at night," he said. The tone of his voice sounded threatening and her anxiety went into overdrive.

"Thanks, again," she replied, picking up her damp bag. She threw it on her shoulder and started walking fast towards the frat house, her eyes darting on either side of her. There was no one out the quad now and the hairs on the back of her neck stood up straight. Instinctively, she turned around to see if he was still there, but the stranger was gone. She exhaled, her fear subsiding a bit. There'd been some students from the university who were reported missing a few weeks ago, and everyone on campus had been on edge ever since. Maybe it was all in her head. When she turned around though, he stood a few feet in front of her, a slight grin on his mouth. How the hell did he get there?

## Read the rest of the Bulwark Anthology!

Bulwark by Brit Lunden

The Knowing, Volume 1 by Brit Lunden

The Illusion, Volume 2 by DJ Cooper

The Craving, Volume 3 by R.L. Jackson

The Window, Volume 4 by E.H. Graham

The Missing Branch, Volume 5 by Kay MacLeod

The Body, Volume 6 by Kate Kelley

The Battle of Bulwark, Volume 7 by Del Henderson III

The Darkness, Volume 8 by Brittney Leigh

If you enjoyed this story, please leave a review on Amazon, Goodreads, or wherever else you love to talk about books. Thank you!

www.ingramcontent.com/pod-product-compliance
Lightning Source LLC
Chambersburg PA
CBHW070507170726
48291CB00008B/2695
*9781947188983*